Edwina Victorious

By the same author
THE SILVER BALLOON

Edwina
Victorious

Story and Pictures by
SUSAN BONNERS

Farrar Straus Giroux / New York

Library of Congress Cataloging-in-Publication Data
Bonners, Susan.
Edwina victorious / story and pictures by Susan Bonners.— 1st ed.
    p.   cm.
Summary: Edwina follows in the footsteps of her namesake
great-aunt when she begins to write letters to the mayor about
community problems and poses as Edwina the elder.
    ISBN 0-374-31968-5
    [1. Great-aunts—Fiction. 2. Letter writing—Fiction.
3. Political activists—Fiction.] I. Title.
PZ7.B64253 Ed 2000
[Fic]—dc21   00-24229

To everyone who ever said,
"Somebody ought to write a letter"
—and then wrote it

Contents

Edwina Victorious

Time Capsule

Edwina's mother signaled for a left turn and pulled into the driveway. "I'm not looking forward to this," she said.

Edwina—Eddy to her family and friends—twiddled one of her corkscrew curls. She wasn't too crazy about this trip herself.

"Can we go in the back door," said Eddy, "like usual?"

"Good idea."

They took the flagstone walk.

Eddy's mother jiggled the key as it caught in the

lock. "I hope I've got the right one." The door swung open into a silent house.

"I don't know why, but I feel like a burglar," she whispered. "It isn't as if we haven't been in Aunt Edwina's house a thousand times."

On the kitchen wall, the grinning cat clock shifted its eyes, while its tail swung back and forth. Eddy had always loved the clock, but it seemed creepy now that Aunt Edwina wasn't here anymore.

"Let's sit down for a moment while I find my list of what needs to be done," Eddy's mother said.

They sat down at the kitchen table. Eddy watched the cat's eyes. Back and forth. Back and forth. Back and forth.

The phone rang.

Eddy nearly jumped out of her skin. Her mother reached for the wall phone. "Hello?" she said in an uncertain voice.

"This is Edwina. Evelyn, you sound as if you've just seen a ghost. Or maybe heard one. I assure you, I'm not that far gone. Now, dear, just sit down and have a nice cup of tea. Then grab a shovel and start heaving it all out. I have everything I want with me here, especially the photos of you and Kenneth and dear little Eddy. I'll see you soon. Bye-bye!" She hung up.

"Well!" Eddy's mother put the phone back in its cradle. "That fall on the garden walk doesn't seem to have slowed down Aunt Edwina, even if it did make her decide to move to Willow Grove Senior Residence." She sighed. "You'd think a ninety-year-old woman would have the sense not to lift a forty-pound bag of potting soil, wouldn't you?"

"She's really going to live at the residence?"

"Sounds like it. She told the *Star-Dispatch* to start running the ad for the house on Monday." Eddy's mother found the tea kettle and began to fill it. "Let's tackle the attic first."

Aunt Edwina was really Eddy's great-grandaunt and the person she was named after. People who thought Edwina was a fragile little bird were soon set straight. She had the handshake of a lumberjack. Until her fall, she'd done her own gardening and firmly rejected family offers to hire a house cleaner. She didn't tolerate a lot of nonsense. In fact, none at all.

Eddy liked that. It almost made it worthwhile to have the awful name. It gave the two of them a special connection. Of course, Eddy didn't have any hope of matching Aunt Edwina's cutting wit. Few people did.

"It's like Arizona up here," Eddy's mother said, as they climbed the attic stairs into hot, dry air.

"Or the mummy's tomb," Eddy said, still thinking of the movie she'd watched last night on Dread Theater.

Her mother got to the top. "Egad. It's more like my Uncle Alvin's junk shop."

Lampshades, suitcases, folding chairs, two fans, three clothing racks, and a trunk were the main features in a landscape of boxes.

Eddy took one look and was ready to go back home. Even her mother seemed daunted. Then she took her customary deep breath. "Well, it's not so bad. Not really."

Eddy admired the way her mother could make light of disasters. She had decided that the ability must come from her parents' business as caterers. Lots of surprises happened in their kitchen, but the best thing was to pretend that nothing was really wrong.

Taking a cue from her mother, Eddy decided to look on the bright side—they might find some amazing thing in the mess.

"We've got to start somewhere," said her mother. She began to make a stack of lampshades. "These will establish our throw-out pile. Eddy, please put them by the garage. We'll make our take-home pile at the back door."

They went after the furniture and appliances first. That was the easy part. The take-home pile took the early lead. Then they turned to the boxes.

For a while, the take-home and throw-out piles ran about neck and neck. Eddy's mother ambled through the contents of each box, exclaiming over any interesting finds. By lunchtime, she'd stopped exclaiming and started to pick up the pace. By three in the afternoon, she was pounding down the home stretch, dispatching boxes at full speed. The throw-out pile began to pull ahead decisively. Eddy lost track of the times she'd gone up and down the stairs.

If the crown jewels were in the attic somewhere, Eddy figured they'd probably get thrown out.

They got down to the last five boxes. Eddy's mother glanced at her watch.

"Good grief. I promised Mrs. Hooper at the thrift store I'd be there by three-thirty with those hideous table lamps from the living room. Can you believe it? She's got a customer lined up for them. Eddy, are you okay here by yourself for a few minutes? You can put on the radio in the kitchen and wait there."

"I'm okay," she called as her mother ran down the stairs and out the back door.

Eddy had a better idea. She was still hoping to find something amazing in one of the boxes that were left. She opened the biggest one. It contained a tablecloth and napkins. Boring. Under that box was a black case with a handle. She snapped open the case and found an old typewriter inside. That was good. Unfortunately, she didn't have any paper to try it out on. She opened a third box.

This one was full of typed letters. They looked like smudged copies, not the originals. All of them were signed "Edwina Osgood."

The one on the top was addressed to "The Honorable Timothy C. Bennett, Mayor" at the Town Hall. But that wasn't the name of the mayor. Eddy looked at the date. The letter was almost forty years old.

Dear Mayor Bennett,

While walking through Walnut Street Park this morning, I was distressed to see the state it has been allowed to sink to. The water fountain has no water. The benches cannot be sat upon. The flower beds are blooming with trash.

Perhaps this is someone's idea of a thought-provoking outdoor artwork commenting on the emptiness of modern life, but I felt as if I had stumbled onto the site of the Mad Hatter's Tea Party.

Parks such as this are not a luxury. They are a necessity. They must be maintained.

Sincerely,
Edwina Osgood

Eddy flipped through some of the other letters. The dates went further back in time as she went down the stack. Each letter was addressed to some important person—the president of the chamber of commerce, the director of the historical society, the chairman of the town council, the head of the library.

Eddy heard their car door slam, then footsteps coming up the walk. She stacked all the letters back in the box, pushed on the lid, and ran down the stairs with it. She put it on the take-home pile and opened the door for her mother.

They worked for another ten minutes, then loaded the take-home boxes into the car.

"What are we going to do with the typewriter?" said Eddy.

"I don't know. It's kind of a dinosaur, but I'd hate to throw it out."

"May I have it?"

"Sure. See if you can find room for it on your side of the car." Eddy's mother pulled out her list and crossed out the first item. "Ta-da! I think we'll let your father do the basement. We shouldn't hog all the fun."

. . .

When they got home, Eddy helped stack boxes on the back porch—all but the letter box. She took that to her room and shoved it under the bed. Fortunately, her mother wasn't that enthusiastic about cleaning, so it was safe there.

She wasn't sure why she was keeping the box a secret. Her mother wouldn't throw it out if Eddy especially asked her not to. Maybe she felt strange because reading somebody else's letters wasn't quite right, even if the person who wrote them didn't seem to care about them anymore.

But this was a chance to find out what Aunt Edwina was like when she was younger. Eddy had seen a photo of her, taken years ago. It showed an athletic-looking woman with short dark hair and a broad smile, sitting on the hood of an old-fashioned car. The brim of her hat was tilted at a reckless angle, almost hiding one eye.

The Aunt Edwina Eddy knew hardly stood taller than her great-grandniece and looked as if a good wind would blow her away. The woman in the photo was a stranger, except for the smile. Eddy recognized the smile. Now she had the letters.

The last thing left in the car was the typewriter. Eddy lugged it up to her room. She hauled out the box and took a handful of letters. The one addressed to the Head of Public Transit caught her eye.

Dear Mr. McCaffery,

As an animal lover, I think it is very considerate of you to provide our local pigeons with a roosting place in the rafters of the train station. By thoughtfully not repairing the broken window near the ceiling these past six months, you are providing an excellent way for our feathered friends to get in.

Unfortunately, as a frequent user of train service, I would like to point out that sitting in the waiting area has become both unpleasant and suspenseful as one wonders what unwelcome surprise may befall one.

Please attend to this matter. The Audubon Society will forgive you.

Sincerely,
Edwina Osgood

Edwina Victorious

The next letter was addressed to the Chief of Police.

Dear Chief Rogers,

As I walked past the baseball field on Monday, I thought perhaps the town zoning laws had changed and that an auto dealership had opened in the west lanes of Poplar Street. This seemed an odd location. On a second look, I realized that I was seeing lines of double- and triple-parked cars. None of them had been ticketed.

On my return trip an hour later, I noticed that the cars were still unticketed. I know they were the same ones because I happened to note a few license plates.

I am sure it is just coincidence, but a number of the cars had stickers identifying the owners as members of the town council.

In the future, will you please educate these unschooled drivers in the parking regulations by issuing the appropriate tickets?

Sincerely,
Edwina Osgood

Time Capsule

As far as Eddy could tell, all the letters were like that. A missing traffic sign, broken steps in a public building, the need for more green space in the downtown area, the lack of funding for new library books—very little seemed to have escaped Aunt Edwina's notice.

Eddy lifted out the entire stack to see the letters on the bottom. The earliest one was more than sixty years old.

She did some arithmetic on scrap paper. Aunt Edwina had written these letters over a period of twenty-one years, starting before she was thirty. Was there another box somewhere? Eddy didn't think so. If these were all of them, why did the letters stop forty years ago?

She put the letters back in the box and pushed them under the bed.

Her father was in the kitchen, preparing for the Garden Club luncheon he and Eddy's mother were catering the next day.

She found him squeezing dough out of a pastry tube, making a line of S shapes on a baking pan. Rows of baked cream-puff shells filled the countertops.

"Dad, you're making the Swan Lake."

"Better believe it. This ought to wow them."

When baked, each pastry S would be pushed into a cream-filled puff, becoming a swan's head and neck. Pieces cut off the top of the puff would be stuck into the cream to form wings. A sifting of powdered sugar turned the swan white.

Then her father would arrange the whole batch of swan puffs on a mirror, with real flowers around the edges. It always caused a sensation.

Eddy climbed onto the kitchen stool and waited until he was done.

"Puffs come out good, Dad?"

"Like clouds. Here, have one." It collapsed in her mouth like a crisp little balloon. The cream filling would go in tomorrow, just in time for the luncheon. "How was cleanup duty?" he asked as he slipped the baking pan into the oven. "Too bad I was tied up here. I was really looking forward to spending the day in a stuffy attic."

"We're saving the basement for you."

"Oh, good. Did you find any Confederate money?"

"She's not that old, Dad."

"Chests full of gold doubloons?"

That reminded Eddy of something she'd once overheard about Aunt Edwina. "Dad, is she rich? Her house isn't like a rich person's house."

"Aunt Edwina, bless her heart, was perfectly happy with the things she had. Anyway, she and Uncle Bert only hit it big the last six or seven years he was alive. Do you remember Uncle Bert at all?"

"Not really. How did they get rich?"

"Piggy Bars."

"Piggy Bars?"

"Best idea since hula hoops. You see, Uncle Bert loved to carve soap. Made little animals and things with a penknife. One day he carved a pig. Something clicked. Make a bar of soap in the shape of a pig— soap for little piggies who play in the dirt all day and need to get clean. And when you used up the soap, you got down to a little plastic pig just right for a farm animal set. But the thing that put it over the top was the oinker."

"The oinker?"

"The little device inside the plastic pig. Made an oink sound when the soap was handled. Kids went crazy for it. Parents went crazy for it because kids went crazy for it. Uncle Bert had to go into mass production. You might say they really cleaned up."

"Very funny, Dad. How come there's no Piggy Bars now?"

"Who knows? Fads come and go. Why aren't people crazy for hula hoops like they used to be?" Her father shook his head. "A real shame he's gone. They don't make 'em like Bertram Farnsworth anymore. The man was a creative genius."

Eddy knew her father would appreciate creativity. His pastries for the catering business were very original, like the birthday cake in the shape of a running shoe with real laces crisscrossed on the frosting. That was a big hit.

"Was Farnsworth Uncle Bert's last name? Why isn't it Aunt Edwina's last name?"

"She kept her own name when she got married. A very independent woman." Her father reached for a broom. "They don't make 'em like Aunt Edwina, either. Having money never changed her, except that now she gives a lot to charity every year. Most people don't know that."

"There's going to be leftover swans, right, Dad?"

"Sure thing. We can't let the Garden Club have them all, can we?"

Home Cooking

The next morning, Eddy decided to ride her bicycle to Fairview Park, two blocks up Oriole Street from her house. Lots of her friends played there. She'd probably meet someone she knew.

A little bird made of cloth and feathers lay on her desk. Eddy's mother had found it in one of the boxes. Eddy was looking for a rubber band to attach it to the handlebars of her bike, when her mother leaned in the doorway to her room. She held out an envelope. "For you from Aunt Edwina."

Eddy had never gotten a note from her great-grand-aunt before. She must have mailed it from the senior residence. The return address was "156 Willow Grove Avenue" and the envelope had a "Willow Grove" postmark, since that was the name of the whole neighborhood.

Dear Eddy,

What a difference a little bag of potting soil can make. Silly of me to have been so stubborn, of course. If my neighbor hadn't come by and found me, I don't know what would have happened.

I did a lot of thinking about that the week I was in the hospital. I decided that the time had come to move on. That's why I came straight here from Community General. If I take another spill, somebody's always around to set me back on my pins again.

Good news—I've graduated from my walker to a cane!

Willow Grove was the right decision. I have my own apartment (wait till you see my kitchenette) and I'm making great headway with the staff. Bill the handyman tells me that most of them roll their eyes when they hear my name. It's a start.

*Enough about me. How are you, Eddy? I miss
you. I know you can visit me here, but it's not the
same as it was when I lived six blocks away.*

*You know, I have great hopes for you. I've always
felt that we share more than a name.*

Come visit soon.

Love,
Aunt Edwina

As Eddy slipped the letter into the top drawer of her
dresser, she wondered what Aunt Edwina meant by
"great hopes."

She went to the kitchen. Her father stood at the
stove tending the big iron pot. Her mother was chop-
ping onions on the counter. The puffs sat on trays,
waiting to be transformed into swans.

"Rush job from the Theater Club," Eddy's mother
said when she saw her. She grabbed another onion.

"Can I go to Fairview Park on my bike?"

"Uh—okay," said her father. "Come back if your
friends aren't there." He wiped his eyes, which were
watering a lot.

"Hot peppers?" Eddy asked. Whatever her father was stirring, some of it was sure to make an appearance at dinner that night.

"Uh-huh. Chili. The Theater Club wants it spicy. I put in lots of hot pepper." He wiped his eyes again.

"No, dear," said Eddy's mother over her shoulder, "I put in the hot pepper." She turned around, a shocked expression on her face. Eddy's father looked up.

"We both put in the hot pepper!" they said in unison.

Eddy thought this was a good time to leave. Her parents would come up with a solution to the problem. They always did.

She strapped on her helmet and maneuvered her bicycle out of the garage. The rubber band worked. With the cloth bird bobbing on the handlebars, she started down the driveway.

Pedaling into the park a minute later, she heard a familiar voice. "Hi, Eddy!"

When she turned around, Roger Bailey was behind her, riding a beat-up bike. He had a white bag in the basket.

Eddy didn't know him very well, even though he'd

sat next to her all last semester. He was quieter than most people and seldom raised his hand, but he usually knew the answer when he was called on.

Eddy stopped her bike. Roger pulled up next to her.

"Hi, Roger. What are you doing over here?" Eddy knew that he lived somewhere across town.

"My mother sent me to get a loaf of bread from Curds and Whey—you know, that health food store on Center Street with all the weird stuff. Do you live around here?"

"Two blocks down Oriole Street."

Roger pointed to the bird on Eddy's handlebars. "That's great. Where'd you get it?"

"We found it when we cleaned out my Aunt Edwina's attic."

"Did she die?"

"No, she fell down and decided to go live in Willow Grove Senior Residence."

"I know that place. I live right around the corner from it. Your aunt must be really old."

"She's ninety. She's really my great-grandaunt."

"I don't know anybody who's ninety. It's lucky you

26

don't live where I do. You'd be stuck visiting her all the time."

"No, I like visiting her. She doesn't seem like she's old. And she's really smart. I wish we did live right next to Willow Grove."

"If you say so." Roger looked as if he wasn't convinced. "Sorry I can't ride bikes with you. After I drop the bread off, I'm supposed to go to the orthodontist to get my braces tightened."

"That sounds awful."

Roger shrugged. "I'm sort of used to it. Well, maybe I'll see you around."

"Yeah, see you," Eddy said.

She watched Roger take off down the path to the far gate. He certainly seemed willing to talk when he had something to say. Eddy steered her bike down the center path. As she came up to the kiddie playground, she saw a little boy toddling along with his mother. He pointed to the baby swings.

"Dah!" he said eagerly, heading for them.

"No, Jason," said his mother. "We can't use those swings."

"Dah?" he said, a furrow on his brow.

A chain-link fence surrounded the swings. Eddy remembered it had gone up just before she'd started school last fall, almost ten months ago. The swings needed repairing. They weren't safe anymore.

The mother took the little boy's hand and pulled him away from the fence. He began to cry.

Eddy hadn't thought about the fence much, but now she was angry. This little boy, and probably lots of others, couldn't have a good time swinging because whoever was supposed to get the swings fixed wasn't doing the job.

Eddy continued on past the playground and circled the park a few times. She couldn't stop thinking about what she had seen. This was the kind of thing Aunt Edwina would have written a letter about. Eddy was angry enough to write a letter herself. But who'd pay attention to a letter from somebody who hadn't even finished grade school yet?

None of her friends was in the park. Eddy went home, stowed her bike in the garage, and opened the kitchen door cautiously. The crisis was probably over, but it was best to be sure.

Her mother sat at the kitchen table, resting her head in her hands and staring at the wall with a dazed expression.

"Everything turn out okay?" Eddy asked.

"Piece of cake," said her mother, not moving. "Have a nice ride?"

"It was all right. Any swans around?"

"Three, just for you. They're in the fridge."

"May I have one?"

"You might as well. Looks like lunch will be late today."

"Is Dad making the deliveries?"

"Yes. I just hope he leaves all the containers with the right clients. Somehow I don't think the Garden Club would appreciate five-alarm chili."

Eddy found the swan puffs and brought one to the table on a plate. Deciding which part to eat first was always half the fun.

"Are we going to visit Aunt Edwina soon?" Eddy

had missed the first two visits to Willow Grove because she'd been in school then.

"Friday or Saturday. How did she sound in her letter?"

"The same as usual."

"In that case, she should be running the place by the time we get there."

Eddy finished her swan. "Need any help?" she said, hoping she knew the answer.

Her mother glanced around the kitchen. "No, I think I'll just clean up with the garden hose and a bulldozer."

Eddy went to her room. She pulled the box out from under the bed and read a few more of the letters. She wished she could write like Aunt Edwina. She'd tell the mayor what she thought about those swings in the park.

Even if she could write like that, the problem was the same. A letter from the grownup Edwina Osgood would be taken seriously. A letter from the young Edwina Osgood would be thrown out. Maybe laughed at, unless . . . unless the person who got it thought it was from the other Edwina.

But anyone who read it was sure to know the truth. "I was distressed to encounter . . . Certainly the town resources are sufficient for . . ." Eddy couldn't think up expressions like that.

What if she copied them? A word from here, a phrase from there—she could cook up something impressive.

She scooped up a handful of letters and took them to her desk. With a little rummaging around, she found a notebook and a pencil. Then she sat down to work.

Where to start? She tried making a list of all the good words and phrases she found. Then she cut up the list and pushed the scraps of paper around like flash cards.

That was no good. Not a single sentence came out that made sense.

She tried copying a single letter complaining about a historic building in need of repair. Each time she came to the words "Avery Theater," she substituted "baby swings."

That was better, but the letter didn't say a thing

about the toddler Eddy had seen. Besides, she didn't think anybody would think the swings were "an irreplaceable cultural landmark."

There was only one solution. She turned to a fresh page in her notebook and began her own letter. When it was done, she substituted some of Aunt Edwina's writing for her own.

She left the heading until last. The return address was easy enough, copied from this morning's note. Then she found an old letter addressed to the mayor and followed the form, putting in the right name. When she reread what she had written, she was quite pleased.

Dear Mayor Granger,

When I was in Fairview Park playground this morning, I was distressed to see the state it has been allowed to sink to.

I saw a little boy and his mother by the baby swings. The little boy wanted to go on the swings, but he couldn't. There's a fence around them thats been there since last September because their broken.

It was really sad because the little boy started to cry when his mother pulled him away.

Why should fixing the swings take so long? Pritty soon that little boy will be too big for those swings.

Such neglect reflects poorly upon our community.

Maybe whoevers supposed to do it forgot about it. That person should be reminded. Please attend to this matter.

Parks such as this are not a luxury. They are a necessity. They must be maintained.

Sincerely,

Eddy closed the notebook and went down to the kitchen. Her mother was putting away the last pans.

"Mom, may I have some paper? I want to type a letter."

"Sure. In my desk, top drawer on the right-hand side. Envelopes are there, too."

Eddy went upstairs to the extra bedroom that her parents had fixed up as an office. She took paper and envelopes for two letters.

Back in her room, she lifted the heavy typewriter

onto her desk, opened the case, and tapped a few keys. The carriage didn't move. Eddy began fiddling with every lever she could find. Suddenly the carriage jumped a space. She rolled a sheet of paper into the machine and opened her notebook to the right page.

Her two-finger typing was slow, but dependable. Line by line, her scribbled words were transformed into an even flow of print. The letter that rolled out looked as respectable as any of Aunt Edwina's. So did the envelope she made.

The signature was trickier. Eddy had to hold one of Aunt Edwina's letters against the window with her own letter on top, then trace the name. The writing came out a little shaky, but it was the best she could do.

Then she handwrote an answer to Aunt Edwina's note.

Dear Aunt Edwina,

Thanks for the letter. I've never gotten one from you before, I guess because we lived so close. Mom says that you have a really nice apartment with a great view.

I hope you don't mind too much not being in your own home anymore. That must be hard to get used to.

We'll be visiting soon. I miss you too.

Love,
Eddy

Stamps were in a dish on her mother's desk. As she sealed the second envelope, Eddy checked the clock. She'd have just enough time to get to the corner mailbox for the last pickup of the weekend. She grabbed the letters and went downstairs.

Passing by the living room, Eddy saw that her mother was sitting on the recliner with her feet up. Her eyes were closed and the magazine had slipped out of her hand. Eddy was used to her parents sleeping at odd times. Sometimes they got up before dawn to start working.

She tiptoed out the back door, then ran to the mailbox. Plop! In went the first envelope, the one to Aunt Edwina.

She reached into the slot with the second letter, the one to the mayor. Lucky that she'd gotten that note from Aunt Edwina this morning, or she wouldn't have known the exact return address to put on the envelope. Suddenly she yanked the letter back.

The postmark. It had to read "Willow Grove," just like the one on Aunt Edwina's note. Willow Grove was across town. Her parents would never let her go that far alone. How could she mail the letter? Roger. He could mail it. If he wasn't dead from his trip to the orthodontist, he could ride his bike over and pick it up.

Eddy tiptoed back to the little office, closed the door, and got out the phone book. She ran her finger down the Baileys. Andrew, John, Michael, Peter— Roger. Maybe Roger was named after his father. She hated calling a number she wasn't sure of, but it was the only way.

She dialed.

On the second ring, a man with a deep voice picked up. "Hello."

"Hello. Is Roger Bailey there?"

"This is Roger Bailey."

"Uh, I meant the other Roger. The one with the braces."

"Oh. Just a minute. I think he was lying down after his appointment with the orthodontist."

Poor Roger. He was a nice person and didn't deserve braces.

He came on the line. "Hello?"

"Roger, it's Eddy. Are you okay?"

"Yeah. I'd like to trade my head for somebody else's, but I'm okay."

"That's good. Can you do something for me?"

"What kind of thing?" He sounded uneasy.

"I need you to mail a letter for me."

A short pause followed. "Eddy, you know those blue boxes on street corners that say United States Postal Service? That's what they're there for."

"No kidding. But this letter has to have a Willow Grove postmark. That's why you have to mail it. If there's a mailbox by the nursing home, that would be the best."

"I suppose there's a good reason for this."

"There is, but I don't want to talk about it now. Let's meet in the park. When can you come over?"

"I'll ask." He put his hand over the receiver. Eddy heard muffled voices. Then Roger came back on the line. "In about an hour. I've got to have lunch first."

"Great. See you."

"See you."

Now the letter would be perfect. Roger was a terrific person.

Eddy heard their car pull into the driveway and the clatter of plates in the kitchen. When she walked in, the table was covered with deviled eggs, shrimp salad, and tiny sandwiches with the crusts cut off.

"Everything but the prize winning begonia," said her mother. "Welcome to the Osgood edition of the Garden Club luncheon."

Eddy's mother seemed a little surprised that she wanted to go back to Fairview after lunch.

"I'm going to meet Roger Bailey there. I called him."

"Roger. Isn't he the one with the overbite?"

"Not anymore."

A few minutes later, Eddy pedaled through the park gate. Roger was already there.

"You beat me."

"Yeah. Lunch goes pretty fast when you drink it through a straw. Where's this letter?"

Eddy pulled it out of her backpack.

Roger looked at the address. "You're writing to the mayor? What's the deal?"

Eddy had intended not to tell anybody, but Roger was doing her a big favor. Besides, he didn't seem the kind of person who'd blab if you asked him to keep a secret.

"You promise not to tell? It isn't anything bad."

She explained to him about the letter she'd written and how she'd traced Aunt Edwina's signature.

"My name is Edwina Osgood, too," she added, "so it isn't a total lie."

Roger looked as if he'd rather have been someplace else.

"The swings need to be fixed, right?" Eddy said. "This is just to remind whoever's supposed to do it."

He took the letter. "Okay. It'll probably get dumped in the wastebasket anyway."

Eddy started to say something and stopped. Roger was right. She didn't know what happened because of Aunt Edwina's letters. Maybe nothing. Maybe the train station window never got fixed, or Walnut Street Park either.

As Eddy watched Roger ride out of the park and turn down Center Street, she wondered if she had wasted her time and Roger's, too.

Mail Call

From his office in Town Hall, Charles "Buddy" Granger watched the traffic go by on Haywood Avenue. He loved looking at his town from this window.

He loved Monday mornings. He loved being the mayor, especially now that he was comfortably settled into his second term.

In a minute or two, his assistant, Harold, would bring in the mail, sorted into three piles. The Immediate Attention stack came from important people, including those very important people who had contributed to the mayor's last campaign. The All in Good Time stack came from concerned citizens who had not contributed to the mayor's last campaign but who would probably vote. The Dump It stack included strangely worded notes scrawled on torn paper and letters from people who would probably never vote.

He swung his chair around to view the photo behind him, a still from his first campaign commercial. Decked out as Paul Revere, he'd climbed on Dapper Dan, an aging saddle horse rented for the occasion. The fact that he'd never ridden a horse before didn't deter Buddy Granger. What an image—the youthful candidate galloping down Main Street at dawn, alerting the community to the dangers of a worn-out administration.

At seventeen, Dapper Dan was in no mood to gallop at dawn or any other time. While the video crew waited, he stubbornly stood his ground. Then a flashbulb exploded. He was off in a dead run. Horse and rider tore past the camera, the frozen smile on Buddy Granger's face a triumph of showmanship over terror.

As soon as the commercial aired, the incumbent mayor gleefully poked fun at it. But Buddy Granger had the last laugh. Come November, he rode Dapper Dan to victory, becoming at twenty-five the youngest mayor in the town's history.

With the oath of office still ringing in his ears, he declared war on neglect. His signature on a succession of memos called up a small army wielding scrub brushes, paint rollers, and jackhammers. He felt like a kid with a new train set.

The town council was caught napping. They woke up soon enough. After his first exhilarating weeks as mayor, the Buddy Granger Express ran smack into a wall.

The council members who favored spending out-numbered those who opposed it—but no two people in the first group could agree on what to spend money on.

The mayor found himself viewing his predecessor with new respect. Running the town at all was a feat, let alone running it well.

However, Buddy Granger was nothing if not a quick learner. A promise here, a favor there—after a rocky start, he began to build a solid record of accomplishment, perhaps not the revolution he had promised, but a solid record nonetheless. Streets were repaved, trees planted, trash collections increased.

Yes, he had pushed through a string of improvements in those early years. If shepherding these projects along no longer held the same interest for him that it did then, that was only normal.

In any case, routine maintenance was best delegated to the appropriate departments. After all, not every broken parking meter merited the mayor's personal attention. A leader had to focus on the big picture and not get bogged down in details, or he'd spend his life filling potholes. Somehow Buddy Granger had always known he was destined for bigger things than that.

Fortunately, at thirty-one, he still had most of his career ahead of him. Who knew where he might be in five years? In ten years? Representative Granger? Governor Granger? Senator Granger? What about . . . Well, time enough to think about that.

His assistant appeared at the door in his customary white shirt and bow tie.

"Come in, Harold!" the mayor boomed. "Let's get this show on the road."

Harold came in balancing three stacks of envelopes and a coffee cup. He deposited everything on the mayor's desk.

"What treasures do we have today, Harold?"

The mayor didn't believe in dawdling. In a few minutes, he had finished off the Immediate Attention stack. The All in Good Time stack went even faster.

"Anything good for laughs here?" said the mayor, fanning out the remaining envelopes.

"No, sir."

"Well then, take it away."

Harold began sweeping the letters together.

"Wait a minute," said the mayor. He picked out an envelope from the Dump It stack and pointed to the return address. "If this 'E. Osgood' is who I think it is, she's a very important person."

Harold flushed deep red. "I'm really sorry, sir. I didn't know."

"No reason you should," said the mayor, shaking the letter out of the envelope. "It's not generally

known to anybody under forty-five, but Edwina Osgood is one rich lady. I met her once, during my first campaign. Sharp—with a tongue to match."

The mayor remembered all too well Edwina Osgood's firm handshake and how she'd looked him straight in the eye. He'd had the uncomfortable feeling that she didn't think too highly of what she saw. He certainly hadn't been able to pry a campaign contribution out of her.

He checked the return address. " '156 Willow Grove Avenue.' I thought she lived on the west side of town. She must have moved. Let's see what she has to say."

Harold read over the mayor's shoulder.

"Sir, for someone who's sharp, aren't there a lot of mistakes in punctuation and spelling? And the signature looks kind of funny. Could this be a practical joke?"

"Hmm. I suppose it's a possibility. We should check this out."

Harold knew that "we" meant him.

"Shall I call Miss Osgood for you, sir, and ask if she wrote the letter?"

"No. If she really wrote this, she'd be insulted that we questioned it. Tactful inquiries, Harold. That's the ticket."

Harold gathered up the mail and headed for the door.

"You understand," said the mayor, "this has top priority."

"Yes, sir." Harold didn't have to ask why.

Back at his desk, Harold pondered where to begin. He decided to walk by the house. Maybe he would find a chatty neighbor.

The walk wasn't a long one. In ten minutes he was standing in front of 156. He had expected to see one of the fine old Victorian homes owned by the town's wealthier inhabitants. Instead, he was looking at Willow Grove Senior Residence.

What luck! His mother's cousin Dorothy worked as a nurse at Willow Grove. He found a pay phone on the corner. Dorothy was on duty. Yes, she could meet for coffee.

An hour later, they were sharing a table at Doodles' Restaurant. Harold asked Dorothy about work.

"Not bad. People can get kind of demanding, but I'm an old hand at dealing with that."

"Um, yes, I suppose some of your residents are a little, um, childlike?" Harold said.

"You could say that," said Dorothy. "Most of the residents are mentally okay, though."

Harold decided to plunge in. "Someone the mayor knows is a resident at Willow Grove. Edwina Osgood."

Dorothy rolled her eyes. "Edwina Osgood is a friend of the mayor?"

"Sort of."

"On top of everything else." Dorothy shook her head. "She'll probably make good on that promise to complain to the state licensing board if we don't get better books in our library."

"Has she been there long?"

"About a month. Seems like a year."

"Is she one of the . . . childlike ones?"

"Yes, if you mean Dennis the Menace. Like yesterday. She slipped past the guard at the front gate and went window shopping on Sayer Street. And that's the second time. The first time, she went to the movies. She said our movie program was strictly for the brain-dead. Said she wanted to see 'an action flick.'"

"So she's strong enough to get around by herself."

"Indeed she is. She needs a cane to do it, and her hands are a bit shaky, but she's got the constitution of an ox."

"I suppose she has family that she phones or, uh, writes to?"

"Well, I don't know if it was to family, but the other day I saw her typing something on an old typewriter that we have for the residents."

They chatted a few minutes longer. Then Harold hurried back to the office and reported his discoveries to the mayor.

"Dorothy described her as Dennis the Menace, sir. That would explain the mistakes in the letter, wouldn't it? She might be, well, going into a second childhood."

Edwina was hardly the sort of person that the

mayor would have pictured experiencing a second childhood. She seemed more like somebody who'd never experienced her first.

But Harold wasn't through. "The signature is easy to explain. Her hands shake. And," he concluded triumphantly, "she was seen using a typewriter a couple of days ago."

"Just a minute. If she's in Willow Grove, how did she get clear across town and see the swings in Fairview Park? I don't believe the residents there are known for long-distance walking."

"She is able to walk with a cane. Dorothy says she went on a couple of excursions. She could have caught the 26 bus and ridden it most of the way."

"I see." The mayor sat forward in his chair. "Harold, I think we'd better do something about those swings. Get me Fred Thompson on the phone. It's time I lit a fire under the Parks Department. What have they been doing with this year's budget?"

"Sir, shall I draft a response to the letter?"

"No. If I know Edwina Osgood, we have to consider

our approach carefully." And, he thought, come armed with a recent accomplishment.

After his assistant left the office, the mayor swiveled his chair to face the window.

He'd certainly heard stories about Edwina Osgood from the veterans of local politics, how at first she'd been dismissed as an eccentric. Until the recipients of her letters discovered that they were dealing with a bulldog. She simply wouldn't give up. Before long, her crisp notes were getting prompt attention.

As far as the mayor knew, she'd dropped out of local politics years ago. But she seemed to have been bitten by the civic-improvement bug again. Maybe now that she had money, she wanted to leave a legacy. Maybe she could be persuaded to provide the funds for some important projects, funds he wouldn't have to pry out of the tight fists of the town council.

So many useful things could be done: the post office restoration, decorative streetlights for the downtown, a new skating pond.

So many ribbons to cut, so many official photos

with the mayor's beaming face squarely in the center—yes, a few generous donations from Edwina Osgood could make a lot of things happen. Then he remembered, Fourth of July weekend was around the corner. The timing couldn't have been better.

The intercom buzzed.

"Yes, Harold."

"Mr. Thompson on the line for you, sir."

The mayor picked up the phone. "Fred, does the word 'pronto' mean anything to you?"

All day Monday, Eddy wondered if the letter had reached the mayor's office and if anybody had read it. But, as the days passed, she thought about it less and less. She went to the pool, to the movies, and to a sleep-over party. Her mother and father catered three luncheons and an awards dinner, so the kitchen was in a constant uproar.

Somehow, everything settled down by Friday and they all went to Willow Grove.

"Darlings!" Aunt Edwina walked toward them with one hand outstretched. The other was on her cane.

Eddy had forgotten about the cane. But Aunt Edwina's grip as she squeezed Eddy's hand was as strong as ever. "How lovely to see you. Let's go sit in the rose garden."

Eddy noticed that a couple of nurses watched closely as Aunt Edwina headed for the door.

"It's all right, girls," she announced with a wave. "No field trips today. I'm too busy." She lowered her voice and leaned over to Eddy. "Ordinarily, I love giving them a thrill."

They found a bench in the shade.

"You look wonderful, Auntie," said Eddy's mother.

"For ninety, I'm a knockout. For anything else, I'm not so sure."

"No, you're looking well," said Eddy's father. "Having all these people to boss around must agree with you."

Aunt Edwina gave a sudden snort of laughter. People on other benches turned to look. "You know, Kenneth, I think you may have put your finger on it."

"So, now that you've had time to settle in, how do you like this place?" asked Eddy's mother.

"Well, it's not home, but I can't expect it to be. Outside of that, it's actually quite a good place. As you see, we have this garden to sit in and a very pleasant sunroom where I plan to toast myself every day next winter. Of course, for what it costs to stay here, you'd expect the Taj Mahal, but this will do nicely. Especially after I've introduced my ideas for a few simple improvements."

"Uh-oh," said Eddy's father.

"For instance, I have in mind replacing some of those rosebushes with raised garden beds that the residents could tend themselves, even if they are in wheelchairs. Roses have their place, of course, but some of us might like to grow a vegetable or two."

Eddy's mother sighed. "Try to limit yourself to one improvement a week. Otherwise, the staff may go on strike."

"I'll try." Aunt Edwina turned to Eddy. "And what have you been up to?"

"Oh, bike riding and going to the pool and reading mystery books and stuff like that." Eddy's heart pounded as if she were telling a lie, even though everything she'd said was the truth.

"Eddy, would you like to see my apartment?"

Eddy nodded, grateful for the change of subject. Besides, she'd been wondering what kind of place Aunt Edwina had.

They all took the elevator to the second floor. The apartment turned out to be small, but sunny and cheerful, with a view of the garden below. Eddy especially liked the tiny kitchenette.

"Great for boiling an egg, which is about the extent of my cooking these days," said Aunt Edwina.

"The cafeteria here is good?" said Eddy's father.

"It's not the Ritz, but it's good. In fact, it's lunchtime now, so I'll go downstairs with you."

They said goodbye on the front porch.

From the back seat of the car, Eddy waved to Aunt Edwina until they turned the corner and she was out of sight.

Say Cheese

The next morning, Eddy was looking for an overdue library book when the phone rang. Her mother called from the kitchen.

"Phone for you, Eddy."

Her mother had been making ginger snaps. The receiver was sticky with molasses.

"Hello?"

"Eddy? Roger. Have you been to the park today?"

"No."

"Well, you better get on over. You don't want to miss the show."

"What's going on?"

"It'll be better if you see for yourself."

Eddy was so excited she ran out the back door.

"Destination!" called her father. "Estimated time of return."

"Helmet!" called her mother.

"Fairview, about a half hour," Eddy shouted as she wheeled her bike out of the garage. "Helmet!" She snapped it on.

As she got near Fairview, she could hear clanking and thumping. A Parks Department truck sat near the entrance. Eddy steered clear of it and rode toward the playground. Part of the chain-link fence had been rolled back. She got off her bike and shaded her eyes to see. A crew of workmen wielding pickaxes and shovels were digging around the baby swings.

A voice came from behind her. "They're digging up the cement anchors that hold the swings down."

Eddy turned. "Roger! I thought you were home."

"I was calling from the pay phone by the gate. It cost me a fortune in dimes to get your number from Information, but I didn't want you to miss this."

"Thanks, Roger. I'll pay you back."

"No, that's okay. It was worth it to be in on the action. Looks like your letter worked."

A terrible idea suddenly occurred to Eddy. "Roger, they aren't going to take the swings out and leave it like that, are they?"

"Didn't you see what was on the truck? Come on. I'll show you." He led the way.

The back of the truck was open, revealing a brightly colored set of brand-new swings. Eddy thought they were the most beautiful things she'd ever seen.

The next Saturday morning, Eddy stood with her parents and Roger in the first row of spectators waiting at the Fairview playground. A wide ribbon was stretched across the entrance. On the other side, the new swings looked wonderful, especially next to the new slide and the new sprinkler. And the border of flowering shrubs was a big improvement on the chain-link fence.

A black car pulled up to a round of applause. The passenger door swung open and the mayor jumped out, smiling and waving as he trotted across the newly installed lawn.

Say Cheese

The head of the Parks Department, who had just lived through the worst week of his life, smiled broadly and pumped the mayor's hand. He praised the mayor's vision and leadership. The mayor spoke glowingly of Mr. Thompson's can-do spirit, the spirit the country was founded on, the spirit of all those who fought for liberty and justice, the spirit that he himself would always seek to keep alive—wherever public service might take him.

Eddy clapped for everything that was said, even the things she hadn't paid attention to. She was very proud.

Someone handed the mayor an enormous pair of scissors. Snip! The ribbon fluttered to the ground amid whistles and more applause.

Sunday morning's *Star-Dispatch*, the regional newspaper, carried a two-column photo of the playground opening. It appeared on page 3 of the second section, "Around the Towns."

Over his coffee, the mayor studied it with a professional eye. As usual, he'd photographed well, the picture of confidence and vigor as he cut the ribbon. Too bad they hadn't run it on the front page, but the coverage was good nonetheless.

At the Osgoods' breakfast table, Eddy's father raised an eyebrow when Eddy pushed aside the comics in favor of "Around the Towns."

"Look, Dad." She held the section up. "We're in the picture."

In the Willow Grove rose garden, Edwina Osgood snapped open the second section of the paper and skimmed the headlines. She glanced at the playground photo and started to turn the page. Then she turned back.

"Look, Mildred." She elbowed the woman sitting next to her on the bench. "That's my great-grandniece. She's quite a girl."

Eddy and her parents went to Fairview Park that evening to see the Independence Day fireworks. As she watched burst after burst of shimmering colors, she decided that this was the best Fourth of July ever.

The next morning, the mayor sat at his desk, trying to compose a letter. The wording had to be just right. It had to trumpet his achievement in the park reno-vation without sounding like boasting. The woman probably had a long hat pin ready to prick anybody's hot-air balloon.

He got up and went past the empty desks to the cof-fee machine. With everyone off for the holiday, the of-fice was silent. He had thought it would be a good place to write the letter.

He sat down again and scribbled a few lines on a legal pad. He crossed them out. He scribbled. He crossed out. He scribbled. He crossed out. He started a new page. He crossed out.

Finally, he crumpled the sheets and threw them into the wastebasket. He'd just have to hope that Ed-wina Osgood read the newspaper.

.   .   .

That morning at the Osgoods', Eddy's mother was in the middle of putting together a very promising lasagna when she ran out of ricotta cheese. Eddy's father was recruited to drive to Ferrara's grocery. It was across town, but Eddy's mother said you couldn't trust anybody else's ricotta.

Eddy asked to go along. Ferrara's smelled good. And Mr. Ferrara insisted on giving out free tastes of his food.

As they drove up Oriole Street with the windows down, Eddy heard squeals and laughter coming from Fairview.

Her father braked and they peered across the ball field to the playground, where three toddlers on the swings were being pushed by their parents. "It's great to see people enjoying the park," he said.

If only he knew how great.

Her father picked up speed again. "I hope Ferrara's will be open today," he said. "It's still the holiday."

"He'll be open," said Eddy. She sometimes wondered if he had another home.

They parked on a side street a block from Ferrara's.

As they walked to the corner, Eddy pointed to the clouds. "They look exactly like swan puffs, don't they, Dad?"

He nodded.

This really was a perfect day. In fact, everything was perfect.

And then she saw the vacant lot.

The space between Ferrara's and Jerrod's Drugstore was paved with cobblestones and might have been the remains of an old street. Its main feature, besides the stump of a dead tree, was a changing exhibit of trash. This morning, a moldy armchair was on display. Eddy knew that it would eventually disappear, only to be replaced by something equally bad.

As far back as she could remember, the lot was like that, but this morning she was especially irritated by it.

They left the brilliant sunshine and entered the mystery cave of Ferrara's. Sausages hung from the ceiling like stalactites. Twisted loaves of bread poked out of baskets. Deeper into the narrow cavern, the formations were mostly cheese.

At the very back, presiding over his wondrous kingdom, was Mr. Ferrara. He greeted them with a smile and a slice of cheese on a spatula. "I got smoked mozzarella. You want to taste?"

Unfortunately, with a lasagna at stake, they had time to taste only five cheeses and two sausages.

"Next time," said Mr. Ferrara with a hint of disapproval, "don't be in such a rush." He reached over the counter and gave Eddy a sesame-seed cookie.

"Mr. Ferrara," she said as he weighed the ricotta, "who owns the lot next door?"

Mr. Ferrara made a face of disgust. "That's town property. I tried to buy it, years ago. I could put some tables there, make a nice café. They won't clean it up and they won't sell it. I give up."

Eddy hadn't been thinking about writing another letter, but maybe she could help Mr. Ferrara. Besides, cleaning up a vacant lot should be easy and hardly cost any money.

As soon as she got home, she sat down with a pad and pencil. Once again, she borrowed phrases from Aunt Edwina's letters to get the right sound.

Edwina Victorious

Dear Mayor Granger,

Thank you for fixing up the Fairview Park playground. Everyone appreshiates it.

Today I would like to draw your attention to a matter that concerns the welfare of our community, namely, the disgraceful vacant lot near the corner of Center and Warren, next to Ferrara's.

Mr. Ferrara is a very nice man who works hard. He sweeps the sidewalks in front of his store two times a day, more if it's windy. He doesn't deserve to have a vacant lot next door, full of garbage. He wants to buy the lot and put a caffay there. You should help him.

Please give this matter your utmost effort.

Sincerely,

Eddy found her mother taking the lasagna out of the oven.

"Look at this lasagna. You could put it on a magazine cover."

"May I have more typewriter paper?"

"Yes, of course, dear." Her mother set the pan on a cooling rack. "Not a magazine cover—an art museum."

Eddy went to type her letter. She found a better pen to trace the signature, so it came out smoother. Only one thing remained to be done. She dialed Roger's number. He answered.

"Roger, will you mail another letter for me?"

A silence followed. Then Roger whistled through his braces, a trick he'd learned that was very impressive.

"You're going to do it again?"

"I hope so."

They arranged to meet at Fairview. Eddy waited anxiously until she saw Roger turn in at the park gate. Watching him ride toward her, she realized that he didn't have a very good sense of balance and that he pedaled slowly. But he got where he was going.

"It's something for Mr. Ferrara," Eddy explained when he took the letter. "You know that vacant lot next to his store?"

"Dump City. Sure, I know it."

"Well, start watching it." Eddy pulled the letter out of the envelope and handed it to Roger. "Let me know if anything happens."

Roger skimmed the page. "If you can get that place cleaned up, Mr. Ferrara will probably give you enough sausage and cheese to last the rest of your life."

"If he does," Eddy said, "I'll split it with you."

Harold waited while the mayor sat drumming his fingers and staring out the window. The letter from Edwina Osgood was on the desk. From time to time, the mayor hummed.

Harold tried not to interrupt—the mayor often hummed while making important decisions—but perhaps some encouragement was in order. "I know the lot, sir. Two guys with a truck could clean it up by the end of the week."

"But we don't want to merely clean it up."

"We don't?"

"We don't. We want to engage in a creative partnership with the business community, Harold. I'll admit, at first I was a bit discouraged by Miss Osgood's response, but she's handed us another opportunity to show what we're capable of. Think café, Harold. Think Old World charm. And get me Jack Murphy on the phone."

At least, the mayor thought as he searched for his aspirin bottle, he knew that Edwina Osgood read the newspaper.

Ten days after the mayor received the second letter, a three-column photo appeared in the "Around the Towns" section. It showed the mayor shaking hands with Mr. Ferrara. Behind them, a group of people, including two children, sat at an outdoor table. The headline read: "Downtown Eyesore Becomes Charming Café."

The accompanying article described the festive umbrellas that shaded the tables, the newly planted saplings, and the tubs of flowers that had transformed the lot, now leased to Mr. Ferrara for a token sum.

It quoted Mr. Ferrara on the turn of events: "Town

Hall—who knows what they do up there? I'm too happy to ask questions, but I must have a friend someplace."

In his office, the mayor examined the photo with satisfaction. He noted the two children in the background. They looked somehow familiar, especially the little girl with the corkscrew curls. Where had he seen her before?

From the Osgoods' home office, Eddy phoned Roger and told him to look at "Around the Towns," page 2. She asked him to meet her at Fairview later that morning.

In the Willow Grove dining room, Edwina Osgood jiggled the tea bag in her cup as she studied the photo. Quite a coincidence, Eddy's being in the paper two times in a month.

A short time later, Eddy and Roger sat watching two babies play by the sprinkler at Fairview.

"Too bad we can't tell Mr. Ferrara who got the lot cleaned up for him," said Roger.

"I know," said Eddy. "But it's got to be our secret for now."

"So what did you want to meet about?"

"Well, I've been thinking. Those letters we sent did a lot of good. Mr. Ferrara is very happy about his café. And look at those kids." The babies were gleefully padding in and out of the water spray. "Lots of other places could be fixed up. If we started looking around, we'd probably get plenty of ideas."

"You mean more letters?"

"Exactly."

Roger thought for a minute. "Sounds like a Secret Santa in reverse—instead of giving things, he'd ask for them."

"But he would give things—he'd make things better for everybody."

"Think it'll work?"

"It's worked so far."

"When do we start?"

"I figure we could start right away."

"We could ride around your neighborhood for a while and see if we find anything," said Roger.

"Good idea."

They didn't see anything. After a while, Roger had to go—another appointment with the orthodontist.

Eddy thought he looked a little deflated.

"Your teeth are going to look great, Roger."

"Thanks. Bye."

"Bye, Roger," called Eddy, as he rode up Oriole Street. "Keep your eyes open!"

Good Deeds

In the following days, Eddy and Roger worked out a system. They each began a list of things that needed fixing up. Every few days, they compared lists and gave each item a rating. "One" had the highest priority. "Two" and "three" had less, in that order.

The graffiti that Roger found on the Veterans' Monument was a definite "one." The muddy patch Eddy saw in Town Hall Park was a "three." The broken sidewalk on Sayer Street rated a "two," along with the grimy bus shelter in front of the library.

Then they made a final decision about which letter

to write next. They established a rule: one subject per letter, no more than two letters in the same week.

Eddy and Roger agreed—they had never had such an exciting summer in their lives. Even a simple trip to the variety store turned into a chance to spot some target for improvement. Finding a good one became a kind of game.

Roger said that watching a location after mailing a letter was better than reading a mystery novel.

"It's not whodunit," he said. "It's more like when-will-they-do-it."

Eddy felt like a fairy godmother. She had only to wave her magic wand and things got done—good things that needed to be done. The feeling was so wonderful she was able to ignore the slight snag of conscience that came and went.

The mayor was not having an exciting time. As July passed into August, Harold's delivery of the morning mail began to seem like an approaching summer storm. The mayor never knew when the lightning would strike, or where.

Edwina Osgood's letters all followed a precise form. After thanking him for his efforts in the previous matter, she would launch into an attack on some new front.

Who was her legman, he sometimes wondered. She had to have one. For a ninety-year-old woman who needed a cane, she was racking up a lot of mileage, with or without buses.

Not that the mayor objected to making the asked-for improvements. They didn't cost much. By now, he was an old hand at slipping new items into existing budgets. In a few short weeks, he had been photographed smoothing cement, scrubbing graffiti, putting up nesting boxes, pushing a broom, and planting flowers. On various occasions, he'd donned a hard hat, rubber gloves, safety goggles, and an apron.

The *Star-Dispatch* duly recorded every event. The week didn't pass without one or sometimes two of the mayor's activities given coverage—but not on the front page.

If Buddy Granger was ever going to see the inside of any office besides this one, he needed something big.

If he couldn't engage Edwina Osgood's interest in a major project that would make banner headlines, he'd be stuck forever in the second section.

The trouble was, the right moment to suggest one of his pet projects never seemed to arise. Instead of steering the course, he had allowed himself to be swept along by Edwina's never-ending torrent of requests.

The mayor was musing on the matter when Harold tiptoed in with the morning's mail. He handed an envelope to the mayor. "I'm afraid it's another one, sir."

The mayor skimmed it and dropped his head into his hands. "She's the fisherman's wife, Harold," he groaned.

"The fisherman's wife, sir?"

"The one whose husband caught a magic fish and threw it back. The fish granted them a wish or two and then the wife got greedy. Started wishing for all kinds of stuff."

"Uh, yes, sir."

As usual, the mayor recovered quickly. "Some cof-

fee, please, Harold. And get me Tom Jacobs on the phone."

The clock tower in front of the courthouse was missing a bronze cherub. Now, who but Edwina Osgood would notice that?

The clock tower had been a gift to the town by a local businessman, long deceased. It featured not only a gaggle of cherubs but also a few birds and some sort of sea creature. The mayor could never make out what it was. One cherub less could only improve the thing, as far as he was concerned, but if Edwina wanted it restored . . .

The official installation of the new cherub took place on the third Saturday in August. At the unveiling, which drew a sizable crowd, the mayor made a mental note to raise Harold's salary. He deserved a reward for tracking down the artist who had sculpted the cherub in the first place. Older than Edwina Osgood herself, he still had a studio on the north side of town. He remembered the project clearly. The original mold was in his basement. In record time, a local foundry turned out a new casting.

The *Star-Dispatch* published a four-column photo of the ceremony on page one of Sunday's "Around the Towns." An editorial proclaimed that the town could once again take pride in its unique clock tower and praised the mayor's efforts in restoring it. The piece went on to laud the mayor for his return to the kind of activism that had characterized his first years in office.

At his kitchen table, the mayor read the editorial with satisfaction. Yes, this was the moment to regain control of the situation, to contact Edwina Osgood and suggest a project somewhat bigger than a cherub.

He turned to the photo. He couldn't believe his eyes. Who was that kid? He reached for the phone, then stopped. Harold would think he was nuts.

At the Osgoods', Eddy's father picked up the second section of the paper. "Hey, Eddy, you and Roger are in the picture again. That's the third or fourth time, isn't it?"

Eddy kept her eyes on the comics she was reading. "Oh, is it?" She didn't bother to phone Roger. She knew he'd see it.

At Willow Grove, Edwina adjusted her reading glasses. That was Eddy all right.

She remarked on it when Eddy and her mother came to visit later that morning.

"So, are you attending ribbon-cutting ceremonies for summer entertainment?"

Eddy thought fast. "Well, Mr. Ferrara had lots of good food at his."

Aunt Edwina laughed. "That's an improvement over most of the ones I ever attended. And I attended quite a few in my time."

"That's right. Weren't you a community organizer of some sort?" said Eddy's mother.

"I had a big mouth, which may be what you heard," Aunt Edwina said. "Unlike my present quiet self."

"What kinds of things did you organize?" asked Eddy.

"I once put together a group to save Town Hall Park. Some people wanted to turn it into a parking lot. Imagine."

Aunt Edwina described a few more of the causes she'd fought for.

"And I used to write letters by the bushel."

Eddy's mother put a hand on Aunt Edwina's arm. "Auntie, I've got to phone Kenneth. He's all alone with a chicken marengo." She went down the hall to the phones.

Ever since Eddy had found the letters, she'd been curious about one thing. Now Aunt Edwina had brought it up.

"Why did you stop writing letters?"

"Who said I stopped?"

"You haven't written one for forty years."

Eddy hadn't meant to say that. It slipped out.

"That's true, but how did you know?"

"I, uh, I found a box of letters when we were cleaning out your attic."

Once she'd said it, Eddy felt better, even though she didn't know what Aunt Edwina was going to say.

"I see. I'd forgotten they were there."

"I'm sorry. I shouldn't have read them."

"No, no, it's all right. I told you and your mother to clean the place out. I knew I didn't have anything that I minded your seeing."

She sat forward in her chair. "Forty years ago, I lost the biggest battle I'd ever fought. Do you know Deerfield, the section on the south side of town?"

"Isn't Deerfield a shopping mall?"

"It is now. It used to be a small community with its own downtown square—beautiful old buildings. Then the state highway commission, in its infinite wisdom, decided to put a highway exit right through the middle of it.

"When we found out that the exit was going to split the community in half and destroy their downtown square, a number of us formed a committtee. I was chairperson. I promised the people in Deerfield that we'd stop the project. We took the matter to court. And we won. But then the highway commission, with the backing of Mayor Bennett and his cronies, appealed the ruling. You see the result—acres of concrete."

"That was only one thing," said Eddy. "You might have won the next time."

"Maybe, but I felt defeated. I turned away from the whole mess, threw out all the letters I'd written for the Save Deerfield Committee. That's why you didn't find any.

"Then I met dear Bertram. I had a job doing research for a patent lawyer at the time and Bert came in for a consultation on one of his inventions. After we got married, I started working with him in his business ventures. Instead of trying to fix everybody else's problems, I began to tend my own garden." Aunt Edwina sighed. "Talking about all this reminds me of how I sometimes felt, knowing I'd helped make things better."

But she *had* made things better this summer, lots of things. She just didn't know it. If Eddy told her what was going on, wouldn't she be happy about the good that had been done?

The slight snag that Eddy had ignored suddenly became a large hook that pulled her up short. She had used Aunt Edwina's name without her permission. That couldn't be right. What should she do?

"Something on your mind?" asked Aunt Edwina.

Eddy tried to sort the tangle of thoughts in her head. She took a deep breath.

Her mother rushed back in. "Kenneth needs help and I can't talk him through it on the phone. Auntie, I'm afraid we'll have to go." She kissed Edwina on the cheek and grabbed her bag. "Come on, Eddy. Seconds count."

Eddy barely had time for a goodbye hug.

After they'd gone, Edwina sat thinking. What had Eddy been about to tell her?

That afternoon, Eddy phoned Roger.

"Another letter?" he asked when he came on the line.

"No, I wanted to talk to you about something."

"Did somebody find out?"

"No. I'll meet you at the usual place."

A short while later, Eddy and Roger found a bench in Fairview Park and sat down.

"Roger, do you think what we're doing is okay?"

Roger didn't answer right away. He watched a sparrow pick up crumbs. "I'm not sure."

"Do you ever feel funny about mailing the letters?"

"I didn't at first. It was fun."

"But you do now?"

"Uh-huh."

"We're not causing anything bad to happen. We're only making sure that good things get done."

"I know. But we're fooling people to do it. I bet they wouldn't like it if they found out."

"Because we're tricking them?"

"Yeah." He scuffed his shoe on the pavement.

"Roger, I've decided. I'm not going to write any more letters."

They rode around the park after that and over to Wally's Ice Cream. Eddy felt much better, good enough to eat an entire double-dip sundae with sprinkles.

Monday was the beginning of a heat wave. People went around saying, "Hot enough for you?" Stories on the weather appeared every evening on the TV news.

Good Deeds

On Wednesday, Channel 27 did a live report from the zoo. Eddy and her father were watching.

The roving reporter was on. "This is Ann Kovacs. I'm here with zookeeper Danny Edwards. With temperatures in the high nineties, workers like him are struggling to keep the animals cool, but it's a big job. How's Snowflake the polar bear faring in this heat, Danny?"

The animal lay sprawled on the cement like a polar bear rug while the keeper sprayed water on him with a hose.

"Well, he's pretty miserable. We're doing the best we can, but he really needs an air-conditioned space for days like this."

"And Snowflake isn't the only one to suffer," the reporter continued. "Our camera caught other residents here doing what they could to beat the heat."

The report switched to videotape showing foxes and leopards panting heavily and a baby llama lying in the bit of shade cast by its mother.

Wherever the camera panned, it showed cramped, barren, old-fashioned cages, not the spacious natural habitats Eddy had seen in magazines and on TV. She hadn't been to the zoo in a while. She'd forgotten what it was really like.

"That's terrible," she said. "Somebody should do something about that."

"They should," said her father. "People bring it up from time to time, but a new zoo isn't in the town budget. They should close the place and send the animals to a decent zoo."

They should. Unless Edwina Osgood could persuade them to fix the one they had.

Later that evening, as Eddy rolled a sheet of paper into the typewriter, she thought about her conversation with Roger. She was going back on what she'd said, but she felt he'd understand. This letter would definitely be the last.

Dear Mayor Granger,

I saw a report on this evenings news that I found very disturbing.

The reporter went to the zoo and talked to a man

who was trying to cool off the polar bear by spraying water on him. The polar bear looked really mizerable. The man said he should have an air conditioned place for days like this.

The other animals they showed looked the same— mizerable.

The worst thing was that all the cages were small with bars and cement floors. Good zoos have natural habitats. Why isn't our zoo like that? It can, and should be, a model for other communities.

By neglecting the needs of others we only diminish ourselves.

Please give this matter your immediate attention.

Sincerely,

Eddy looked at the clock. She'd have to wait until morning to phone Roger.

Picture This

On Friday morning, the mayor arrived at the office early, anxious to make up for lost time. He had intended to contact Edwina Osgood right after the cherub unveiling, but his plans had been sidetracked. On Monday, a water main had broken, flooding the intersection of Center and Sayer. Since then, the mayor had been on the phone nonstop, supervising repairs and reassuring store owners.

This morning, he was going to dictate that letter no matter what. But which project should he pitch first? He kept changing his mind.

His assistant paused in the doorway, envelopes in hand. The mayor motioned him in.

Silently, Harold handed over the Edwina Osgood letter.

The mayor took it as if he were being offered a handful of poison ivy. What little duty did she have in mind this time? Would he wind up scrubbing the Town Hall steps, or planting petunias in the park? He started to skim the letter. Maybe he'd wind up polishing the flagpole or . . .

The zoo! Of course, the zoo. What a stupendous idea!

"Harold, we've got it." The mayor showed him the letter. "This is the break we've been waiting for. And it's her idea."

"Sir, I don't see anywhere in the letter where she says she'll pay for it."

"A minor obstacle at the moment. The main thing is, she's interested. Now, how do we keep this ball rolling?"

They considered the problem.

"Meet with her in person?" suggested Harold.

"Definitely. But remember, she probably has a tight hold on her purse. Can we create a situation where she'll be carried along by the excitement of the moment and make a commitment on the spot, preferably in public?"

"Can we?"

"I believe we can. What do you think—a visit to Willow Grove with press coverage. Lights and cameras. And a representative from the zoo." The idea grew in his mind by the second. "And animals. People love animals." The mayor made a mental exception for himself. He had never gotten on well with the four-footed.

"Won't that disturb the other residents?"

"They'll love it. It'll be a break in a boring routine. Does Willow Grove have a space where we can stage this?"

"I believe they have a rose garden, sir."

"Excellent!" The mayor liked the sound of it. Rose garden. White House rose garden. "We'll set up chairs and invite them all." He reflected briefly on the large voter turnout among the elderly. He planned to shake a lot of hands.

"I'll thank Edwina Osgood for the concern for our town expressed in her letters. Then I'll move on to her concern for the animals as well." The mayor's voice rose dramatically. "We'll describe the kind of zoo we could have—enclosures without bars, greenery like the Amazon, air-conditioning, ponds. A waterfall, why not?"

"That's thrilling, sir."

"Thank you, Harold. Then we'll move on to the thorny part."

"The money?"

"The money—if only we had the money." He sat back in his chair. "Well, what do you think, will she bite?"

"She's got to."

"Good. Better get right on the arrangements. Set it up for Tuesday if you can."

Harold suppressed a gasp.

"Meanwhile," continued the mayor. "I've got a letter to dictate."

· · ·

After that, Harold's day quickly turned into a whirl-wind of phone calls. Getting permission for the event from the head of Willow Grove Senior Residence was only the first hurdle.

Dr. Alfred Fletcher had trouble grasping why the mayor would want to hold a press conference about the zoo at a senior residence, especially since Harold thought it best not to mention Edwina Osgood just then. But Dr. Fletcher readily understood the value of publicity in attracting new business. Of course, Willow Grove was available.

Harold contacted the newspaper, the local TV station, people who provided chairs and tables, and, of course, the zoo.

Yes, the director of the zoo could attend. The animal was more of a problem. Knowing the mayor's discomfort around animals, Harold decided that only one animal should appear and that one should have previous TV experience. This limited the number of candidates.

Picture This

Harold's first choice, the koala, was about to have a baby. The ostrich was being treated for a foot infection. The lynx had been in a bad temper that week, and the black bear cub had the sniffles. That left only one possibility.

"A tapir is available, sir." Harold stood at the mayor's desk with a clipboard full of notes.

"What's a tapir?"

"It's a hooved mammal native to South America and the Malay Peninsula."

"Do they bite?" The mayor remembered all too vividly his ill-advised photo op with the baby cougar.

"I don't think so, sir. They're herbivores."

"Herbivores have teeth, Harold." He sighed. "Just make sure it's on a short leash."

Edwina Osgood glanced up as a bird flew past the dining-room window. Then she took another sip of tea and reread the letter that had arrived that morning.

Edwina Victorious

Dear Ms. Osgood,

Let me take this opportunity to thank you for all the letters you have sent me this summer. Your many, many suggestions were well taken, and I hope you were pleased to see them put into action. The town is indebted to you.

I want you to know that I share your great desire to have a new, modern zoo.

However, my experience in government has taught me the wisdom of seeking public support before going ahead with any project. In the interest of fostering this support, I would like to hold a press event at Willow Grove on Tuesday afternoon at 2:00 p.m. Channel 27 will carry live coverage.

If you are agreeable to this arrangement, please notify Dr. Alfred Fletcher and he will pass along the information to me.

Let's do it for the animals.

Sincerely,
Charles Granger

Edwina's first reaction had been to wonder if the mayor had taken leave of his senses, or if she had. What letters?

She knew her wits were intact, and the mayor, whatever his shortcomings, seemed like a competent man. As far as she could see, he'd learned a lot in his six years in office.

So he'd received letters, apparently from her, letters that suggested various actions to benefit the town. They sounded much like the letters she used to write—the letters Eddy found in the attic.

Her great-grandniece certainly seemed to be taking an unusual interest in civic affairs this summer. Edwina had the pictures to prove it.

Didn't it all add up to one conclusion? Their shared name was the frosting on the cake.

Edwina thought back to Eddy's last visit. Now she knew what her great-grandniece had been about to tell her. Well, she'd better give her another opportunity. She went to her room and dialed the number.

"Evelyn? Edwina. I know you were here last Sunday,

but that visit got cut rather short. Can you and Eddy stop by tomorrow? Wonderful. I'll see you in the morning, then. Goodbye, dear."

Edwina opened the top drawer of her dresser and took out the newspaper photos that she had saved. Paging through them, she began to chuckle. Eddy had certainly kept the mayor hopping this summer.

As Eddy walked up Willow Grove's front steps with her mother on Sunday morning, she had one of her more serious attacks of stomach butterflies. Ever since Aunt Edwina's phone call yesterday, she'd been in a turmoil.

Aunt Edwina was in the garden. After a few minutes' pleasant chat, she pulled out a change purse. "Evelyn, would you do me a big favor? Do you know Hansen's Bakery?"

"It's down the street a few blocks, isn't it?"

"Yes. I've been dying for one of their strudels. Would you be an angel and bring us a few?" She held out a ten-dollar bill, which Eddy's mother politely refused. "Eddy can stay here with me."

The butterflies in Eddy's stomach did a figure-eight maneuver.

After her mother had gone, Eddy and Aunt Edwina sat in silence for a while, watching a chipmunk scurry back and forth.

"Aunt Edwina? I've been meaning to tell you something. The playground in Fairview Park—that got fixed up because I wrote a letter to the mayor."

"Oh."

"And Ferrara's café. That happened because I wrote another letter."

"Who would have thought," said Aunt Edwina innocently, "that a couple of letters could have such a big effect?"

"Well, see, the mayor thought the letters came from you."

"Now, why would he think that?"

"I suppose," Eddy said, "because I copied your signature and put 156 Willow Grove for the return address."

"That would do it," said Aunt Edwina.

"I'm sorry, Aunt Edwina. I shouldn't have done that

without telling you. But all those things the mayor did this summer—fixing the broken sidewalk and the new cherub and all that stuff—he wouldn't have done them if he knew I was writing the letters."

"No, I suppose not. My money makes me important to him." She paused. "I know you wanted to do good, Eddy, and you did. But you took something from me when you did it."

At first, Eddy wasn't sure what she meant. "Your name?"

"Yes. You put words in my mouth that I never said. Of course, I'm glad all those things got done, but that brings me to another point. You could have asked me to write the letters in my own name. I would have been happy to do it. After all, it's been a long time since I needled anybody in government. I don't want to lose my touch entirely."

"I already made up my mind after we visited last Sunday," Eddy said, "not to write any more letters. And I didn't—except one, after I saw the zoo animals on TV. Somebody has to do something about it."

"It certainly looks that way," said Aunt Edwina.

"About the letters—you know that this matter has to be straightened out, don't you, Eddy?"

Eddy nodded.

"I think," said Aunt Edwina, "you'll have a chance to do that on Tuesday."

"Strudels all around!" Eddy's mother came down the garden walk with a white box.

"Evelyn," said Aunt Edwina, as they passed the box around, "I got a letter from the mayor yesterday."

"The mayor?"

"Yes, I met him during his first campaign. I think he wants to renew the acquaintance. Seems he's planning a little shindig for the press on Tuesday at two o'clock, right here at Willow Grove. It'll be carried live on Channel 27, no less. Can you and Kenneth and Eddy be here?"

"Well, Kenny and I are facing a Chamber of Commerce dinner on Tuesday, so we're stuck at home. But I'll bet Eddy would love to come, right, Eddy?"

Eddy had been listening to Aunt Edwina with growing panic. Press? Live TV? This was the chance Aunt Edwina was talking about?

"Uh, sure."

"Good," said her mother. "We'll get you a ride with the car service."

"Wonderful!" said Aunt Edwina. She gave Eddy a sharp look. "Then I can count on you."

That afternoon, Eddy phoned Roger. "I wanted you to know, I told my Aunt Edwina about the letters."

"Was she mad?"

"No. She wasn't too happy about it either, but she didn't get mad."

"Is she going to tell anybody else about it?"

"No, but I am. She said I should straighten this out. I'm pretty sure that's what she meant."

"You mean you're going to tell the mayor?"

"I think I sort of have to. There's going to be some kind of meeting at Willow Grove Tuesday afternoon. The mayor's going to be there. I'm supposed to go. It's going to be on Channel 27."

"You're going to do this on TV?"

"Uh-huh."

"Are you scared?"

"Uh-huh."

"Maybe you should write down what you want to say and read it, in case you're nervous."

"That's a good idea. Roger, I'm not going to tell that you mailed the letters."

For a minute, Roger didn't say anything.

"But I helped," he said. "Maybe they wouldn't have believed the letters if the postmark had been wrong. Nothing would have gotten done."

"You don't want to get in trouble, do you?"

"No. But I wouldn't mind if people knew that I helped with the playground and Mr. Ferrara's café and all the other things."

"Roger, you have to make up your mind. Should I tell or not tell?"

"Tell. They probably won't send us to prison for more than ten years."

"Very funny."

"What time is this thing going to be on TV?"

"Two o'clock."

"I'll be watching."

Garden Party

On Tuesday afternoon, Eddy stood at the entrance to the Willow Grove rose garden, uncertain where to go. Folding chairs had been set up in two sections, with an aisle between them. A number of the chairs were already occupied.

"Over here, Eddy!" Aunt Edwina waved to her from an aisle seat in the first row. "I was told to sit here."

"I like your hat," she added, as Eddy took a seat next to her.

"Thanks," Eddy said, pulling the bill of her baseball cap down a little farther. She checked her watch again.

Garden Party

One forty-five. The program couldn't last more than an hour. By three o'clock, the misery would be over.

She hadn't told her parents about the speech she was going to make, but she knew they planned to have the TV on in the kitchen. She tried not to think about the unpleasant surprise they were about to get.

Meanwhile, people were rushing all over the garden, setting up lights, lugging cables around, and testing microphones. A few feet in front of her, someone set a jug of water with ice cubes on the speakers' stand. Eddy had no idea that putting on a TV program was this complicated.

A few residents were still being escorted across the lawn by nurses who kept looking left and right as if they were crossing a busy highway. Any second, they might be run down by someone carrying a heavy piece of equipment.

The mayor wasn't in sight. After attending the ribbon-cuttings this summer, Eddy knew that he always breezed in at the last minute, looking in command of the situation.

As she slumped down in her chair, Eddy felt a reassuring pat on her shoulder.

"Don't worry," said Aunt Edwina. "Everything is going to work out fine. Oh, look." She pointed. "Isn't that the most remarkable creature you ever saw?"

Coming down the garden path, held closely on a leash by a young man, was an animal that Eddy had never seen before. It appeared to have been put together from three or four different animals. Its body was that of a large pig, but its legs were too long for a pig's. The feet belonged to a small rhinoceros. The nose was a very short elephant's trunk. Whatever it was, it seemed disturbed by all the activity.

Forgetting her nerves, Eddy watched in fascination as the young man tried to find a safe place to park the animal.

"Put him there," Aunt Edwina called to him, pointing to a space in the line of rosebushes just behind the speakers' stand. "Nobody will bother him there. What is he?"

"He's a tapir," the young man called back. "His name is Kiki."

He backed his charge in between two rosebushes. This shelter seemed to calm the animal, which quietly began eating a rose.

"Look at that," Aunt Edwina said to Eddy. "Roses are good for something after all."

The frenzy of activity subsided to a buzz. Eddy glanced behind her. Some of the residents seemed puzzled, but most of them were watching the proceedings with great curiosity.

"Fred, is that a potbellied pig?" someone said.

"Can't be, Walter," said the man sitting next to him. "Snout's too long."

Eddy turned to face the front. The woman who had done the live report from the zoo positioned herself next to the speakers' stand, holding a microphone. Another young man, this one in a white shirt and bow tie, stepped up and addressed the crowd.

"Thank you all for coming today. The mayor will be here any minute. I think you'll find this will be an interesting afternoon. We're sorry to clutter your garden with all our equipment, but we'll have everything back to normal very shortly."

He stepped aside. A man wearing headphones faced the reporter, who watched him intently. Eddy could hear him counting.

"Ten, nine, eight . . ." The reporter held the microphone up. " . . . three, two . . ." She smiled. "One."

"This is Ann Kovacs, and I'm reporting live from Willow Grove Senior Residence. At any moment, the mayor will be arriving. We understand that he will be accompanied by the director of the zoological park. Word from the mayor's office is that they will talk about the need for a complete renovation of the zoo. And here is the mayor coming down the path with Mr. Frobisher."

The rapidly approaching figures startled the tapir. It withdrew into the foliage.

Unaware of anything unusual, the mayor directed Mr. Frobisher to his seat in front of the rosebushes and stepped up to the stand. He checked out the crowd. That had to be Edwina Osgood, sitting next to the kid in the baseball cap.

"Good afternoon to all of you. What a beautiful day we have to talk about an extremely important topic."

The tapir reemerged and began nibbling the sleeve of Mr. Frobisher's elegant suit. Mr. Frobisher, whose primary qualification for his job was being a classmate of the council chairman, watched in growing alarm.

"We have with us today a man who speaks for those who cannot speak, for the creatures who share our planet and enrich our lives, who are a never-ending source of delight and wonder. I refer to Mr. Frederick Frobisher of our zoological park."

The mayor turned to Mr. Frobisher. Then he saw the tapir. For an instant, the mayor went blank. The creature looked like nothing he'd ever seen before.

"—a never-ending source of wonder. I give you Mr. Frederick Frobisher."

Mr. Frobisher, who was only too glad to leave his chair for the safety of the speakers' stand, motioned the keeper to bring the tapir forward. The mayor stationed himself well away from the strange beast. From time to time, he eyed it suspiciously.

Mr. Frobisher introduced Kiki and briefly described the habits of the forest-dwelling tapirs of the Malay

Peninsula. Then he turned to his main theme, contrasting the present woefully inadequate zoo with the world-class zoo that could be had—with sufficient funding. He finished to a round of applause.

The mayor stepped forward. "Thank you, Mr. Frobisher. Now I would like to highlight the contributions of a very special person who's done a lot for our community in her lifetime. She's kept a low profile these last few years, but this summer she's back in action. It was thanks to her that many projects were brought to my attention, including the Fairview playground and Ferrara's café. With her constant stream of letters, she's kept our office on its toes and we're all grateful to her. I refer to your fellow resident, Edwina Osgood."

To Eddy's horror, the spotlights were suddenly turned on the front row aisle seats. Another round of applause broke out. Carrying a microphone, the mayor came over and shook Aunt Edwina's hand. She smiled and took the microphone.

"Thank you for the introduction, Mr. Mayor, but

I'm afraid you're thanking the wrong Edwina Osgood for the letters. You see, I didn't write any letters this summer."

The mayor looked as if he'd been hit with a brick.

"But," she continued, "the person who did write them is here, and I think she has a few words to say."

A murmur went through the crowd. Eddy stood up.

"The cap," whispered Aunt Edwina.

Eddy reached for the brim and pulled, releasing a mop of corkscrew curls. The mayor's jaw dropped. She was the one? The letters that ran him ragged all summer came from this kid?

"It was me," she said quietly.

Aunt Edwina handed the microphone to Eddy and motioned her to face the audience.

Eddy cleared her throat twice. "My name is Edwina Osgood. The other Edwina Osgood is my great-grand-aunt." With her free hand, Eddy unfolded a sheet of paper from her pocket and started reading from it. "This summer I wrote letters to the mayor. I asked him to put up new swings and clean up a vacant lot. I traced Aunt Edwina's signature and used her return address, so the mayor would think they came from her. My friend Roger mailed them for me from the mailbox out front so the postmark would be right." Eddy's voice started going hoarse. She cleared her throat again.

"Then we found some more things to ask for. Roger and I only asked for things that would help people, but . . ." She lost her place on the paper. "But . . ." She stuffed the paper back in her pocket and looked at the audience.

"Using somebody else's name is telling a lie. And Roger said he felt funny about mailing the letters after a while because we were fooling people. Keeping it a secret wasn't much fun because we couldn't tell people like Mr. Ferrara what we'd done. We decided not to send any more letters. Excepting I decided to send one about the zoo.

"I want to tell the mayor and Aunt Edwina that I'm sorry. And my parents. And I want to thank Aunt Edwina for not getting angry and yelling. And thanks, Roger, for helping me decide what to do."

For a moment, no one reacted. Then Aunt Edwina

stood up and took the microphone from Eddy. "I always knew my great-grandniece was quite a girl, and today she's proved it. The mayor was right about a few things. I was very active in community affairs and then quit, forty years ago, after a big disappointment. But now I'm getting my hand back in." She shot the major a quick look.

"I'm very interested in this zoo renovation," she continued, "now that Eddy's made me aware of the situation. I'm going to start a fund for it and be the first contributor. I think when they see my check, both the mayor and Mr. Frobisher will be pleased. And I plan to encourage contributions from those of my friends who are in a position to be generous. But, be warned, I intend to keep a close eye on every expenditure down to the paper clips." She handed the microphone back to the mayor amid loud applause.

For the first time that anyone could remember, the mayor seemed to be at a total loss for words, but he found his way back to the speakers' stand like a homing pigeon going to its roost.

"This is—we are—let's all give a hand to Edwina

Osgood for this welcome announcement." He picked up stride. "This is the spirit that will renovate, not just the zoo, but our whole community." He made a sweeping gesture meant to embrace that whole community. Instead, it caught the water pitcher.

Two quarts of water and ice poured onto the unsuspecting Kiki. The keeper felt a yank as the leash went taut and he was dragged down the center aisle.

"Easy, boy, easy!"

Snap! The rivets in the leash gave way. Kiki was loose.

In pursuit went Harold, the keeper, Mr. Frobisher, and the feature reporter from the *Star-Dispatch*. Keeping well ahead of the pack, the panicked animal began to do laps around the audience. Harold spun around for an interception, but Kiki swerved and kept on going. Mr. Frobisher tripped on a cable and a spotlight went crashing into some rosebushes.

The head nurse rushed to the front. "Look to the residents!" she shouted to her staff. Her voice was drowned out by cheering and laughter from the audience. Kiki was clearly favored.

While Mr. Frobisher limped to the nearest chair, the keeper tried Harold's interception strategy again. This time, Kiki pulled up short and took off for the far corner of the garden, straight for the low spot where rain had left a mud puddle. Kiki slid onto his side, scrambled to his feet, then slid onto his other side. The keeper made a flying tackle. Kiki slipped through his arms like a stick of butter. Harold pounced. The feature reporter made a grab. Kiki squealed and pulled away.

Fred slapped Walter on the arm. "I thought I'd seen my last greased-pig contest when I left Oklahoma!"

"My money's on the pig!" shouted Walter.

Second for second, the camera man from Channel 27 stayed with the action. This was the best day of his career.

Meanwhile, the photographer from the *Star-Dispatch* snapped away.

The mayor sensed he'd better take charge. He steered a surprised Ann Kovacs in front of the camera and began his own interview. "Well, these unexpected things do happen, Ann, but the residents here seem to be enjoying the afternoon."

The cameraman panned the audience. Now they were looking left to right and left again like people watching a tennis match. Glancing over his shoulder, the mayor saw that Kiki was tearing back and forth, trampling the line of rosebushes behind him.

"Come on, Eddy," said Aunt Edwina, "let's get in on the fun." She grabbed Eddy's hand and marched up to Ann Kovacs. "Ann, I have to hand it to the mayor," she said, pulling the microphone in her direction. "This is much more exciting than I thought it would be."

A cheer went up as Kiki wiggled out of another tackle.

"And I want to say," she continued, "when I met the mayor some years ago, I thought he was a bit of a lightweight. But he's matured in office. In my opinion, he's a fine mayor and we're lucky to have him."

Ann Kovacs turned to the mayor. "That's quite an endorsement, Mr. Mayor. What's your reaction?"

"I think it's a good thing I have Edwina Osgood on my side."

Aunt Edwina pulled the microphone to herself again. "I would also like to mention that this would be the ideal time for Willow Grove to take my suggestion and put in raised garden beds for the residents to plant vegetables. I mean, now that the roses will have to go."

The cameraman panned the flower beds. Not a rosebush was left standing.

Roger Bailey adjusted the TV aerial. He was really glad Eddy had written that last letter. Otherwise, the Great Tapir Race would never have happened.

Of course, he had to do some explaining to his parents. If the *Star-Dispatch* printed all the things Eddy had said, maybe that wouldn't be so bad.

In the Osgoods' kitchen, Eddy's parents stared at the TV screen. On the stove, the rice pudding quietly boiled over.

"Kenneth," Eddy's mother said at last, "I think we've been spending too much time in the kitchen."

"I think you're right, Evelyn," he said.

In the back room of his grocery, Mr. Ferrara turned down the volume on the TV and wiped the tears from his face. He couldn't remember when he'd laughed so hard. Now, that was his idea of a press conference. Usually these things were so dull.

He'd have to make up a nice basket of sausages and cheeses for Eddy, and one for Roger, too.

As the mayor rode home in his official car later that afternoon, he reflected that, overall, things had gone quite well. He had his commitment from Edwina Osgood for a healthy donation to the zoo. That was the main thing.

There was the garden to restore, but that was a minor matter. And Harold had once again proven his resourcefulness by capturing the tapir. Of course, that hadn't been difficult once the animal had jumped into Mr. Frobisher's lap.

Only one thought disturbed the smooth surface of his mind. Now he had two Edwina Osgoods to deal with instead of one.

Starting Over

The front-page banner headline in Wednesday morning's *Star-Dispatch* announced the news—"Mayor Swings Deal for New Zoo!" "Local Benefactor to Kick Off Fund Drive with Generous Contribution" was the cheerful subhead.

The five-column photo featured Kiki in midair, diving straight for the lap of the astonished Mr. Frobisher. "Press conference tapir's off" read the caption.

The mayor knew somebody would have to make a pun on the word "taper." Why couldn't the zoo have sent a nice quiet iguana? Well, no matter. He had what he wanted. He settled back in his chair and took in the view of Haywood Avenue. This was going to be a beautiful day.

Edwina Osgood put down her newspaper and watched a squirrel darting around the remains of the rose garden. At Willow Grove, she'd thought that she'd be closing the book. Now, thanks to Eddy, she was opening a whole new chapter. No question, her instincts about Eddy had been right. Her great-grandniece was justifying the hopes she'd had for her.

Eddy phoned Roger to meet her at Fairview.

"Did your parents watch the press thing on TV?" she asked when they'd found a bench in the playground.

"They caught it on the late news. Channel 27 showed your speech again. I heard about it at breakfast. At least, the surprise had worn off by then."

"What did they say?"

"My dad asked how I'd like it if somebody was using my name, which I wouldn't. He said we were lucky that your aunt was nice about it, and the mayor, too,

or we could have been in real trouble. My mom said it sounded to her like I'd figured that out for myself. What did your parents say?"

"Some of the same stuff, and that they were glad I'd told the truth. My mom said they were sorry they'd been so busy all summer. They should have known something was going on." Eddy was silent for a moment. "Roger, I'm sorry if I got you in trouble with your parents."

He shrugged. "It's okay. They aren't angry now."

Something seemed different about Roger. Suddenly Eddy realized what it was. "Roger, you're not wearing your braces."

"The orthodontist took them off last Saturday. I've just got this retainer." He grinned to show it.

"I told you your teeth would look great."

"Thanks."

After that, they talked about school starting in a week and what teachers they hoped to get.

"Do you think you'll miss the excitement?" Roger said.

"Well, I'm going to be helping Aunt Edwina on the

zoo project. She wants me to get information for her on how to create natural habitats."

"Where are you going to find that?"

"I'm not sure." Then Eddy had an idea. "You could help, Roger. You're good at finding things like that. Mr. Albright really liked your report on yak herding in Mongolia."

"Sure. I'd like to help. I wouldn't have to mail any letters, would I?"

"No letters."

They agreed to meet at the library on Friday. Then Eddy had to leave.

"School clothes," she explained. "We're going down-town. We'll stop and see Aunt Edwina on the way."

"Tell her I saw her on TV," said Roger, climbing onto his bike. "Tell her she ought to have her own show. See you."

Eddy waved and started for home. As she turned down Oriole Street, she noticed a gaping hole in the fence around the ball field.

She'd have to send the mayor a letter about that.